little Miss Neat

by Roger Hargreaves

Little Miss Neat was a very tidy person.

Probably the tidiest person in the world.

She lived in Twopin Cottage.

It was called Twopin Cottage because she kept it as neat as two pins!

She just couldn't stand a mess.

Every day she spent all day polishing and dusting and cleaning and making sure that things were in their proper places.

One morning Little Miss Neat awoke in her bedroom at Twopin Cottage.

She looked out of her bedroom window.

It had been raining during the night, and there was a puddle in the middle of her garden path.

"Oh," she gasped in horror, and rushed outside with a duster.

She mopped up every drop of puddle, and then she rushed inside and washed the duster, and then she ironed the duster, and then she folded the duster, and then she placed the duster very neatly back in its drawer.

Everything in Twopin Cottage had its proper place!

Now, this story is about the time Little Miss Neat went on holiday.

She always went away for one week every summer, and this year was no different.

She spent two weeks packing.

And then she spent a whole day polishing her suitcase.

And then off she set leaving Twopin Cottage all spick and span and neat and tidy.

"Oh I hope it doesn't get too dusty while I'm away," she thought as she closed the door behind her.

But something worse than dusty was going to happen to Twopin Cottage.

Would you like to know what?

Mr Muddle came to tea!

He'd written to Miss Neat to tell her, but, being Mr Muddle, he somehow got into a muddle posting the letter.

Actually, what happened was that when Mr Muddle went to post the letter he had the letter in one hand and a half-eaten sandwich in the other.

And you can guess what happened, can't you?

That's right!

He posted the sandwich!

A posted cheese sandwich!

"It'll be nice seeing Miss Neat again,"
he chuckled to himself as he walked home.

"This sandwich is a bit chewy," he thought.

It was the day after Miss Neat left that Mr Muddle arrived.

He walked up the garden path of Twopin Cottage, and knocked at the door.

No reply!

"Goodbye!" he shouted.

It should have been "Hello!" but he isn't called Mr Muddle for nothing.

"Nobody home?" he called.

He pushed open the door.

"Oh dear," he thought as he looked around.

"Nobody home!"

"Never mind," he thought. "I'll make myself a cup of tea and wait for Miss Neat."

So he went into the kitchen of Twopin Cottage, made himself a cup of tea, and waited.

And waited.

And waited.

And waited.

And went home.

Little Miss Neat stepped out of the taxi outside Twopin Cottage.

"That was a lovely holiday," she said, paying the taxi driver. "But it's nice to be home."

She walked up the garden path, and went in through the door.

"Not too dusty," she said to herself looking around.

"I think I'll make myself a nice cup of tea before I start unpacking."

But, making tea after a Mr Muddle visit isn't quite as easy as it sounds.

Little Miss Neat eventually found the teapot.

Not in its proper place.

In the refrigerator!

And she eventually found the milk.

Not in its proper place.

In the teapot!

And the tea.

In the sugar bowl!

And the sugar.

In the milk jug!

And a cup.

In the oven!

And a saucer.

In the breadbin!

But, could she find a teaspoon?

She could not!

The telephone rang.

Little Miss Neat picked it up.

"Hello", she said.

At the other end of the line Mr Muddle suddenly realised he was holding the telephone the wrong way round.

He turned it the right way round.

"Goodbye," he said.

"Who's that?" asked Miss Neat.

"It's you", replied Mr Muddle.

Miss Neat thought.

"It's Mr Muddle, isn't it?" she guessed.

"Yes," replied Mr Muddle, getting it right for once.

"And you paid me a visit while I was away on holiday, didn't you?" she guessed again.

"Yes," replied Mr Muddle, getting it right for twice.

"Can I come and see you now you're back?"

"I suppose so," sighed Miss Neat.

"Goodbye!"

"Hello!" said Mr Muddle.

And put the 'phone down.

Little Miss Neat sighed a heavy sigh, and sat down in the armchair next to the telephone.

Ouch!!

She looked underneath the cushion.

There were all her teaspoons.

And knives!

And forks!

I don't think Little Miss Neat will be taking a holiday next year.

Do you?

Fantastic offers for Little Miss fans!

Collect all your Mr. Men or Little Miss books in these superb durable collectors' cases!

Only £5.99 inc. postage and packing, these wipe-clean, hard-wearing cases will give all your Mr. Men or Little Miss books a beautiful new home!

Keep track of your collection with this giant-sized double-sided Mr. Men and Little Miss Collectors' poster.

Collect 6 tokens and we will send you a brilliant giant-sized double-sided collectors' poster! Simply tape a £1 coin to cover postage and packing in the space provided and fill out the form overleaf.

STICK £1 COIN HERE (for poster only)

Only need a few Little Miss or Mr. Men to complete your set? You can order any of the titles on the back of the books from our Mr. Men order line on 0870 787 1724. Orders should be delivered between 5 and 7 working days.

───── TO BE COMPLETED BY AN ADULT ─────

To apply for any of these great offers, ask an adult to complete the details below and send this whole page with the appropriate payment and tokens, to: MR. MEN CLASSIC OFFER, PO BOX 715, HORSHAM RH12 5WG

☐ Please send me a giant-sized double-sided collectors' poster.
AND ☐ I enclose 6 tokens and have taped a £1 coin to the other side of this page.

☐ Please send me ☐ Mr. Men Library case(s) and/or ☐ Little Miss library case(s) at £5.99 each inc P&P

☐ I enclose a cheque/postal order payable to Egmont UK Limited for £..................................

OR ☐ Please debit my MasterCard / Visa / Maestro / Delta account (delete as appropriate) for £..................................

Card no. ☐☐☐☐ ☐☐☐☐ ☐☐☐☐ ☐☐☐☐ ☐☐☐☐ ☐☐☐☐ Security code ☐☐☐

Issue no. (if available) ☐ Start Date ☐☐/☐☐/☐☐ Expiry Date ☐☐/☐☐/☐☐

Fan's name: .... Date of birth: ....

Address: ....

....

.... Postcode: ....

Name of parent / guardian: ....

Email for parent / guardian: ....

Signature of parent / guardian: ....

Please allow 28 days for delivery. Offer is only available while stocks last. We reserve the right to change the terms of this offer at any time and we offer a 14 day money back guarantee. This does not affect your statutory rights. Offers apply to UK only.

☐ We may occasionally wish to send you information about other Egmont children's books.
If you would rather we didn't, please tick this box.

Ref: LIM 001

cut along the dotted line and return this whole page